OLIVER TWIST

Written by **Charles Dickens**
Illustrations by **Pini Sposito**

스푼북

IN THE WORKHOUSE

Oliver Twist was an orphan. His mother died on the very day he was born. No one knew who his father was. He was given the surname 'Twist' by the beadle. The beadle,

whose name was Mr Bumble, was a kind of church policeman. He was responsible for finding homes for orphans, and making sure they were taken care of. But Mr Bumble didn't have much time for children.

Oliver grew up in a baby farm. This was a place that looked after young children without parents. The local church paid for their care,

but they didn't pay very much –
certainly not enough for toys, cakes
or Christmas trees, or any of the
things that children enjoy.

A woman called Mrs Mann ran the
baby farm. She was selfish, and kept
most of the money she was meant
to spend on the children for herself.
As a result, the children were always
hungry and only had old, torn clothes,
that were always too big or too small.

By the time Oliver Twist was nine years old, he was a pale, thin child. But on the inside he was clever, kind and spirited. Now he was nine, he was too old to stay at the baby farm.

Mr Bumble came to take Oliver off to the workhouse. This was where poor people were fed and sheltered – though not well – in exchange for work.

Oliver's job was to unpick old tar-covered strands of ship's rope so the fibre could be used again. It was boring, and it hurt his hands.

Oliver and the other boys who worked there were fed in a large stone hall. There was a great copper bowl at one end, and the workhouse master

ladled gruel out of it at mealtimes.
The gruel was a sort of watery
porridge. The boys were allowed one
ladle of gruel, no more. It was all they
ate, except on special occasions when
they each got a small piece of bread.

For months, Oliver Twist and his companions slowly starved. At last, they got so desperate that they decided someone had to speak up – someone had to ask for more food. The task fell to Oliver Twist.

The evening arrived, and the boys took their places. The master, in his cook's uniform, stationed himself by the copper bowl.

The gruel was served.

The gruel was eaten up, every last watery drop of it.

The boys whispered to each other, and winked at Oliver. Two of them nudged him. Oliver was desperate from hunger and misery. He rose from the table, bowl and spoon in hand, and walked up to the master.

'Please, sir, I want some more,' he said.

The master turned very pale. He gazed in shock at Oliver for some seconds. The boys in the hall were shaking with fear.

'What?!' bellowed the master in disbelief.

'Please, sir,' replied Oliver, 'I want some more.'

The master hit Oliver on the head with the ladle, and shrieked for Mr Bumble.

The beadle dragged Oliver off to the gentlemen who ran the workhouse. They all looked well fed and well dressed, unlike Oliver.

These gentleman were in a very important meeting when Mr Bumble entered. He announced with a roar, 'I beg your pardon, sirs! Oliver Twist has asked for more!'

Every face looked round in horror.

'For *more*!' said one gentleman who was wearing

a white waistcoat. 'Do I understand that he asked for *more* after he had eaten his ration of supper?'

'He did, sir,' replied Bumble.

'This boy will be come to a bad end,' said the gentleman. 'I know he will.'

They ordered Oliver to be locked up overnight. The next morning a poster was put up outside. It offered five pounds to anybody who would take Oliver Twist away with them.

Soon enough, they found someone willing to take Oliver. Mr Sowerberry was an undertaker. He was a tall, gaunt man, dressed in a threadbare black suit.

He thought Oliver could be useful to him, sweeping and cleaning in the workshop where the coffins were made.

Mr Sowerberry was not an unkind man. In a way Oliver's life with him was better than in the workhouse, even though he had to sleep in a room full of half-built coffins. On the other hand,

Mr Sowerberry's wife lived up to their name. She was sour and bad-tempered, and didn't like Oliver at all.

There was another young assistant called Noah who thought he was  far better than Oliver. He teased and mocked the young boy by calling him 'Workhouse' and insulting Oliver's mother. 'She was a bad 'un,' he said, 'a regular right-down bad 'un.' Oliver could not remember his mother.

16

He didn't even know her name, but he was very protective of her.

One day Noah's teasing and taunting went too far and they fought. Oliver won. Noah complained to Mr and Mrs Sowerberry.

The Sowerberrys faced Oliver like judges.

'Noah called my mother names,' said Oliver. 'That's why I hit him.'

'So what if he did?' said Mrs Sowerberry. 'Your mother deserved what he said, and worse.'

'She didn't,' said Oliver.

'She did,' said Mrs Sowerberry.

'It's a lie!' shouted Oliver.

Mrs Sowerberry burst into a flood of tears. Mr Sowerberry was forced to take action. He hit Oliver several times, and then sent him off to bed in the coffin workshop.

Once he was by himself, Oliver decided that there was nothing for him here.

No family.

No future.

He had to escape.

At Fagin's

As the first rays of the sun struggled through the shutters in the workshop, Oliver got up. He quietly unlocked the door to the street and then paused.

Left or right?

He turned left, walked up a hill, and then

cut across some fields. He passed
Mrs Mann's baby farm with a
shudder, and arrived at a high road.
He sat down by a milestone.

It said: LONDON 70 MILES.

But, that was alright. Oliver was determined to seek his fortune far away.

He survived the next few days thanks to the kindness of a road-mender, who gave him some bread and cheese, and an old woman, who gave him a little money.

On the seventh morning, Oliver limped into the town of Barnet,

near to London. He sank down on a
doorstep. He was exhausted.

After a time, he noticed a boy of
about his age staring at him. The
boy was short, with a snub nose and
sharp little eyes.

'Hello!' he said to Oliver. 'What's
the news?'

'I'm very hungry and tired,'
replied Oliver. 'I have been walking
for seven days.'

'Walking for seven days!' said the
boy. 'Then you'll want some grub,
and you shall have it.' He bought
Oliver some ham and a loaf of bread
at a nearby shop. Oliver discovered
his new friend's name was Jack

Dawkins. Although most people called him the Artful Dodger.

'Going to London?' asked Jack.

'Yes,' said Oliver.

'Got anywhere to stay?'

'No.'

'Money?'

'No.'

'I've got to be in London tonight and I know a respectable old gentleman who lives there,' said Jack. 'He'll give you somewhere to sleep for nothing.'

Jack and Oliver spent the whole day walking to London. By seven o'clock that evening they arrived in a particularly dirty part of the city. The streets were narrow and muddy. Men and women lounged

in doorways. Babies screamed
inside the run-down houses, and
children scurried about everywhere.

Oliver was thinking of running
away again, but then Jack grabbed
him by the arm and steered him

into one of the houses. A rough-
looking man stuck his head out of
a door at the end of a passage. He
was holding a candle. There was a
woman behind him.

'Why, it's the Dodger,' the woman
said.

'Hello, Nance,' said Jack.

'There's two of you,' growled the
man. 'Who's the other one?'

'A new pal,' said Jack. 'Is Fagin
upstairs?'

'He's sorting out the loot,' said the
man.

The two boys climbed a dark,

rickety staircase. At the top, Jack
threw open a door. The room
behind it was black with dirt and
soot. Sitting around a table were
four boys of about Oliver's age.
Against the far wall there were
beds made out of old sacking.

A wrinkled old man was cooking sausages with a toasting fork by the fire. He had matted red hair and wore a greasy coat.

'Fagin,' said Jack to the old man, 'this is my friend, Oliver Twist.'

Fagin made a bow in Oliver's direction.

'Very glad to see you, my dear,' he said.

The boys welcomed him too. They shook his hand, helped him take his coat and hat off, and even tried to empty his pockets for him. This help was not necded as Oliver's pockets were empty.

The table was littered with handkerchiefs. Fagin noticed Oliver staring at them and said: 'We've just got 'em out ready for the wash, that's all, Oliver. Ha ha ha!'

Was this the 'loot' the man downstairs had mentioned?

Oliver was confused but, above all, he was hungry. He ate his share of the sausages with gusto. The food, together with the long day's walk, made him drowsy. He sank down on one of the piles of sacking. Soon, he was sound asleep.

The boys were out of the room most of each day. They were friendly. It was almost as if they were all

part of one big family. They came
back with assorted items like
handkerchiefs, wallets, watch chains,
and sometimes even watches.

Fagin would examine all
these items, and sometimes
praise the boy who'd
brought them for his
workmanship. He
got very angry if
a boy came back
with nothing,
however.
How did they
have the time

to make these things? Oliver didn't know.

Oliver was a little frightened of Fagin, even though the old man was giving him food and shelter. He was much more frightened of the man downstairs, whose name was Bill Sikes. Sikes had a violent temper. The boys often heard the sounds of arguing between him and the woman, who was called Nancy.

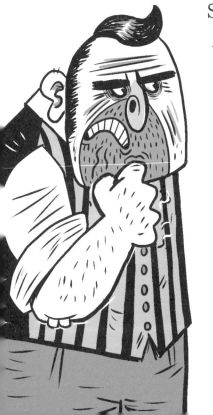

Like everyone, Nancy was
frightened of Sikes, but she seemed
to love him too. She was kind to
Oliver. She smiled at
him and asked him
how he was doing.
Oliver wasn't sure
how to answer, but
it was nice to be
asked.

From things he overheard, Oliver realised that Sikes and Fagin were in business together. But what kind of business?

Oliver found the answer about a week after he'd first arrived at Fagin's. He was out walking with Jack, whom he now called the Artful Dodger like everone else, and a boy called Charley.

Suddenly the Dodger stopped.

'See that gent by the bookstall?' he said. 'The one in the green coat?'

'He'll do,' said Charley.

Oliver stood and watched as his friends crept up behind the man in the green coat. He was reading a book from the stall.

Oliver was horrified to see the Dodger plunge his hand into the gentleman's pocket and draw out a handkerchief.

In an instant Oliver realised just what it was the boys did each and every day. This was where all the handkerchiefs and notebooks and watches came from.

His new friends were pickpockets and thieves!

Oliver stood there, both horrified and amazed.

Unfortunately, the gentleman reached for his pocket at that very moment and saw what was happening.

The two boys ran as fast as they could.

So did Oliver.

But he wasn't as quick or experienced as the others.

By the time the cry 'Stop thief!' went up, the Dodger and Charley vanished. But Oliver was hardly round the first corner when he was knocked down by a huge man. A crowd gathered. Oliver lay on the ground covered in mud and dust.

The crowd parted to let through the gentleman from the book stall and a police officer.

'Yes,' said the gentleman, 'that is the boy.' But he did not look angry. He was staring at Oliver as if

trying to remember where he'd seen
him before.

The officer seized Oliver by the
collar and dragged him up.

'It wasn't me, sir,' said Oliver.

'That's what they all say,' said the
officer.

At Mr Brownlow's

The next few hours passed in a blur. Oliver was taken to a police station, and then to court. The only witness to the robbery was Mr Brownlow, the gentleman whose handkerchief had been stolen.

But instead of accusing Oliver of being the thief – or one of the thieves – Mr Brownlow said that the boy was innocent.

The case was dismissed and Oliver was told to go. When Mr Brownlow left the courtroom a few moments later, he saw Oliver lying on the pavement, white-faced and trembling.

'Poor boy!' said Mr Brownlow, bending over him. 'Someone call a cab, quickly.'

Oliver, hardly aware of what was happening, lay on the cab seat. Mr Brownlow clambered inside. Despite the clatter of the cab and the thud of the horse's hoofs, Oliver fell asleep.

Oliver woke in a warm, comfortable bedroom. An old woman was looking at him. He tried to sit up, but she said softly: 'Hush, my dear. You must be quiet or you will be ill again.'

'Have I been ill?' he asked.

'You've had a fever, but the worst is over.'

The door opened and a man walked in. Oliver recognised Mr Brownlow. He smiled to see Oliver awake.

He came to the bedside and looked at Oliver. But all he said was: 'You have got some colour back in your cheeks, I'm glad to say.'

Over the next few days,
Oliver recovered his strength.
He discovered he was in John
Brownlow's house. The old lady
was his housekeeper. They were
very kind people, and they were
espccially concerned about Oliver.

Oliver was fed well and allowed to sleep in as late as he liked. He was treated better than ever before in his life. Mr Brownlow even bought him a fresh set of clothes.

Sometimes, Oliver had nightmares about his past life. He said nothing of this to Mr Brownlow or the kindly housekeeper. As far as they were concerned, Oliver was safe and happy now.

One day, Oliver was with Mr Brownlow in the study. It was full of books and there were pictures on the wall. One of the pictures was of a beautiful lady. Something about her face was familiar, though Oliver did not know exactly what.

Mr Brownlow looked slowly at Oliver, then at the portrait. He shook himself and started talking about the books in the room. Oliver would read them one day, he said.

Mr Brownlow clapped his hand to his forehead suddenly.

'What's the matter, sir?' said Oliver, who was very respectful to the man who had rescued him.

'Good heavens, I never paid him!' said Mr Brownlow. 'That

book is still in my coat pocket.'

In the confusion over the theft of his handkerchief at the bookstall, Mr Brownlow had slipped the book he was reading into his pocket. He had never paid the bookseller. Mr Brownlow was horrified. He needed to pay at once!

'I'll go, sir,' said Oliver. He was desperate to do something nice for the man who had been so kind to him. 'If you'll trust me with the money, that is.'

'Of course I trust you, Oliver. But you have been ill, you know. You shouldn't be running about.'

'I'm better now,' said Oliver.

It was true, he was better and felt stronger than ever before. Mr Brownlow gave him five pounds and a letter for the bookseller.

With the money and note tucked in his new jacket, Oliver set off through streets he hadn't trodden for several weeks.

AT FAGIN'S AGAIN

Fagin and Bill Sikes hadn't forgotten Oliver. Sikes had plans for the boy. Sikes's speciality was breaking into rich people's houses at night. Oliver was a small boy, just the right size to slip through a narrow window where bigger boys might get stuck.

Yes, Sikes had big plans for Oliver.

Fagin and Bill were also worried. They knew Oliver had been arrested and dragged to the magistrates' court. They knew he had then been taken to Mr Brownlow's because a couple of Fagin's boys had run after the cab to see where it was going.

What they didn't know was what Oliver was saying. He wasn't a hardened thief like the Dodger or Charley. Those boys would have kept their mouths shut. But Oliver Twist might give them away at any time! He could even lead the police to their front door!

They had to get their hands on Oliver before he did any damage. As long as the boy was at Mr Brownlow's, he was safe. But the moment he was back on the street ...

As it happened, Oliver was already back on the street.

In fact, he was racing through the streets. He thought only about paying the bookseller and racing back to Mr Brownlow's with the change. He wanted to show how reliable and trustworthy he was.

Suddenly he heard a woman cry: 'It's Oliver!'

He recognised Nancy's voice before he saw her face. Too late he realised that Bill Sikes was with her. Sikes seized Oliver by the arm and started to drag him away. Nancy looked sorry to have called out Oliver's name.

To the passers-by, who looked as though they might ask questions, Sikes growled: 'This here's my boy.'

They half ran, half stumbled back towards the dirtier, poorer part of town. Oliver would have broken free if he could but Sikcs's grip was too tight. They were soon outside Fagin's lair.

They made their way through the dark hall, up the rickety staircase, into the sooty room.

Fagin was sitting at the table examining the usual handkerchiefs. His tangled red hair hung down either side of his face. Charley and a couple of other boys were lounging in the corner.

'I got him,' said Sikes.

'I am glad to see you again, my dear,' said Fagin.

 'What you been doing, Oliver?' asked Charley.

Oliver said nothing. He thought about Mr Brownlow. The kindly gentleman would be waiting for him to come back from the bookshop. When he didn't, Mr Brownlow would think he had taken the money and run away. In Mr Brownlow's eyes, Oliver would definitely be a thief.

That thought was almost worse than being back in the hands of Fagin's gang.

'Nice new rags you're wearing,'
said Sikes, feeling Oliver's coat.

'And lots of brass too,' said
Charley, extracting the five pounds
from Oliver's pocket.

'Must be your reward for blabbing about us,' said Sikes.

'It's not mine,' said Oliver.

'No, it's ours now,' said Charley.

'Who did you tell about this place?' demanded Sikes.

'N-n-no-one,' stammered Oliver.

Fagin snatched the coins away from Charley. Then the old man gripped Oliver's shoulders, with his claw-like hands. He bent low and whispered in Oliver's ear, 'Just tell us, my dear.'

'I haven't said a thing,' said Oliver.

This was true.

Nancy had been standing by silently. Now she said: 'Oliver wouldn't blab.'

'Hold your tongue, Nance,' said Sikes. 'Speak when you're asked.'

Sikes and Fagin went over to the fireplace and talked quietly. Then Fagin said to the whole room: 'It's not safe here anymore. We're going to Jacob's Island.'

Jacob's Island

Jacob's Island was a piece of land near the London docks. It was surrounded by a muddy ditch that filled with water when the tide was in, making it a sort of island. Ramshackle old houses crowded Jacob's Island. They were so old

that half of them had already fallen down while the other half seemed about to sink into the ditch – including the gang's new hideout.

No one came here if they could help it. It was the safest place that Fagin and Sikes knew. The other boys came and went, but Oliver wasn't allowed to leave at all. He was kept in an upper room. There were two doors, but they were both locked. A window looked over the muddy ditch. It was so tiny that even Oliver couldn't squeeze through it.

Nancy brought him bread and cheese with an occasional scrap of meat.

'What's going to happen to me?' he asked her.

In answer, Nancy put her arms round him. Oliver thought she was crying. This made him afraid for her … and for himself.

Sometimes he heard voices arguing downstairs. Mostly it was Bill Sikes's voice, and once or twice it was Nancy's.

Three or four days passed like this. Then, one evening, as the sun

was going down, the noise below
reached a new pitch.

Sikes was shouting and raging.

Nancy shrieking.

Then there was a sudden clatter
and a thump. It sounded as if
something – or someone – had
fallen down hard.

Now, there was a sinister silence.

Oliver put his
ear to the door.
He could hear
nothing but the
rapid beating
of his heart.

He went to the tiny window. There
was a rickety bridge across the ditch
outside. It wasn't much more than
a few planks tied together. The light

was low but Oliver saw a group of men crossing the bridge one at a time towards the house.

There was a thunderous banging at the front door. Shouts of 'Open up!' bellowed through the woodwork.

A frantic scrabbling of keys unlocked the door to Oliver's room. The Artful Dodger leapt inside.

'What's happening?' said Oliver, panicked.

'It's the traps,' said the Dodger.

'Traps' was their slang word for the police.

'Bill thought Nance told the police 'bout this place so Bill's gone and–'

The rest of the sentence was drowned out by the banging and shouting from downstairs. It grew louder with every second.

The Dodger ran to the other
door, produced a key, and slipped
through it as quick as lightning.

Oliver never saw him again.

Heavy steps came rapidly up the
stairs. It was Bill Sikes's turn to
burst into the room.

His hair was stuck up in spikes and he was carrying a coil of rope.

Sikes looked at Oliver as if he'd never seen him before in his life. Then Sikes shoved him so hard in the chest that he fell down.

Sikes stopped for a moment in the doorway where the Dodger had made his escape.

Beyond him, Oliver could see the evening sky.

Sikes said: 'Every rat's got to have a hole to go to, eh, boy?'

The doorway led to a small ledge between the roofs of neighbouring houses. Sikes looked around desperately, trying to decide what to do next. He made a noose out of the rope and aimed it at a chimney stack.

He was going to try to lower himself into the ditch, which was now full with water from the returning tide.

Oliver heard police down below. They had been joined by a shouting crowd. It was impossible to tell whether they were cheering Sikes on or jeering at him.

From the doorway, Oliver saw Sikes's black figure silhouetted against the sunset sky.

83

He saw him throwing the noose of the rope towards the chimney. He saw the loop fall short. Sikes lost his footing and tumbled off the edge of the roof.

There was a roar from down below.

Then there was absolute silence.

HOME

Oliver was once again at Mr
Brownlow's. This was where he would
stay now. It was to be his home.

It turned out that Nancy had
gone to John Brownlow.
She had feared for
Oliver's life

once he'd been taken to Jacob's Island. John Brownlow alerted the police to Fagin's hiding place, but it was Nancy who paid the price.

Sikes had accused her of betraying them. He had killed her.

Oliver often thought of Nancy – of how she had risked everything to save him. He was glad the Artful Dodger had got away. Glad, too, in a way, that Fagin had been arrested.

But there were new things to think about now.

One day, Oliver was in Mr Brownlow's study. He was gazing at the picture of the strangely familiar, beautiful young lady.

Mr Brownlow removed it from the wall and brought it closer for Oliver to see. He studied the two side by side, the boy's face and the young lady's.

'You do not see the likeness?' he asked. 'Ah well, the one person you cannot see is yourself, Oliver. Here, take the picture.'

Mr Brownlow explained that the woman was Oliver's aunt. Mr Brownlow had been meant to marry her. Sadly, she had died before the wedding could take place. But she'd had a much younger sister

called Agnes whom Mr Brownlow remembered fondly.

Though he lost touch with Agnes, he knew she had fallen on hard times and later had a child. Mr Brownlow tried time and time again to find that child. He had given up hope when, one day, a group of boys tried to rob him at the bookstall.

'The moment I saw you, Oliver, I knew there was something familiar about you. Even though you were covered in dirt and about to be taken away by a police officer. But I could not be sure. I had to make enquiries. I spoke to people from your past who knew more than they told you about your mother. And just when I was certain, you disappeared into Fagin's hands again.'

As Mr Brownlow talked, his voice began to tremble.

Oliver did not reply straightaway. He could not. He traced the image of the lady's face in the picture with his finger. She was the link between him and his mother. His mother, Agnes.

At last he knew her name.

Charles Dickens

Charles Dickens was born in Portsmouth in 1812. Like many of the characters he wrote about, his family were poor and his childhood was difficult. As an adult, he became known around the world for his books. He is remembered as one of the most important writers of his time.

Illustrations by
Pipi Sposito

Pipi Sposito was born in Buenos Aires. He's always been painting. As a child, he enjoyed making figures out of building clay, and when he was older, he started designing for humor magazines. He was surrounded by the original paintings of many experimental artists, and he painted various styles out of curiosity. His illustrated books include 《A Christmas Carol》《A Tale of Two Cities》《Great Expectations》《Oliver Twist》.

OLIVER TWIST

초판 1쇄 발행 2023년 6월 27일

글 찰스 디킨스 | 그림 피피 스포지토

ISBN 979-11-6581-437-3 (74840)
ISBN 979-11-6581-418-2 (세트)

발행처 주식회사 스푼북 | **발행인** 박상희 | **총괄** 김남원

편집 김선영·박선정·김선혜·권새미 | **디자인** 조혜진·김광휘 | **마케팅** 손준연·이성호·구혜지

출판신고 2016년 11월 15일 제2017-000267호

주소 (03993) 서울시 마포구 월드컵북로 6길 88-7 ky21빌딩 2층

전화 02-6357-0050(편집) 02-6357-0051(마케팅)

팩스 02-6357-0052 | 전자우편 book@spoonbook.co.kr

제품명 Oliver Twist
제조자명 주식회사 스푼북 | **제조국명** 대한민국 | **전화번호** 02-6357-0050
주소 (03993) 서울시 마포구 월드컵북로6길 88-7 ky21빌딩 2층
제조년월 2023년 6월 27일 | **사용연령** 8세 이상
※ KC마크는 이 제품이 공통안전기준에 적합하였음을 의미합니다.

⚠ 주 의

아이들이 모서리에 다치지
않게 주의하세요.